MEMORIES OF TOMORROW

MEMORIES OF TOMORROW

Women of the Ozarks

THE SCRAPBOOK SERIES, A PREQUEL

NATALIE R. VICE

Felsenthal Publishing
Tuscaloosa, AL

Distributed by Bublish, Inc.

Paperback ISBN – 978-1-64704-112-0
eBook ISBN – 978-1-64704-113-7

CONTENTS

Dedication ix

CHAPTER 1 1
CHAPTER 2 7
CHAPTER 3 13
CHAPTER 4 17
CHAPTER 5 20
CHAPTER 6 22
CHAPTER 7 25
CHAPTER 8 29
CHAPTER 9 34
CHAPTER 10 38
CHAPTER 11 42
CHAPTER 12 47

About the Author 49
A Note from the Author 51

Women of the Ozarks
The Scrapbook Series

Memories of Tomorrow, A Prequel
Tomorrow's Promise
Crossing Yesterday
Unraveling
The Other Side
Wait For Me...

Discover more at
www.facebook.com/NatalierVice

www.natalievice.com

This book is dedicated:

To every woman who's ever looked in the mirror and realized that time has taken its toll.

To every woman who's ever needed a friend.

To every woman who's given everything to her family.

To every woman who's made difficult, life altering choices for another's sake.

To every woman who's ever looked back with regrets.

To every woman who faces each day with hope in her heart, and kindness on her lips.

Sometimes life gives us magic, something that cannot be explained or reasoned, something or someone that changes the course of our life; call it luck, call it fate, or call it love. Families and true friends bring us magic moments that we collect and remember forever.

-Unknown

Once upon a time... there were these two girls...

These two girls grew up in the Ozarks of Arkansas and Missouri...
These two girls grew to be as close as sisters....
These two girls grew into women....
These two girls grew apart....
These two girls grew older....

And now, these two girls need to find a friend.

CHAPTER 1

Wednesday, May 19th, 2012, Gina Remembers...
6:30 am

THE MORNING SUN ROUSED Gina from a fitful slumber. She'd spent the last few pre-dawn hours hovering between reality and anxious dreaming of so many long-forgotten yesterdays. Her final dream was a mere haze... a blurred vision of the sun glinting off a 737.

Only the gleaming sun wasn't a dream. Those blinding rays really were pouring in through her bedroom window, and slowly pulling her out of those last few moments of a drowsy vision of Jo, Little Rock, and yesteryear.

Suddenly, Gina's mind snapped to life. Today was the day! Today she and Jo were going to spend a few hours catching up, looking back, and in the process figure out if there was anything left of the friendship they'd known. At least that was Gina's purpose in sending out the friend request. She needed her old friend. In fact, she desperately felt she needed her old friend. But so much time, so many years had passed; was it even possible to go back?

Almost as suddenly as the dawning day's reality had leapt upon her drowsy mind, the feelings of nervousness swept again through her body and mind. The reunion with Jorja today had created a real sense of unease; it was as if anticipating the reunion took her back to those schoolgirl days, and a schoolgirl's doubtful mind took possession of an otherwise logical and self-confident woman.

And, as if on cue, all the reasons that things might not go well swirled through Gina's mind. She knew them by heart. She knew the conversation that played out in her mind, word for word. She'd been visiting those thoughts everyday for the last week.

"My life has been so boring…so stuck-in-the-mountains-boring. Jo's traveled the world. What could we possibly still have in common?" I can't think of a thing we still have in common… once we get past all those "back in the day" memories, what will fill the silence?

She's educated, smart, and I'm, I'm… really what am I? A tired old woman that does her best to help counsel and rehab drug addicts. Boy, that's going to make for a great conversation.

We can't swap kid stories; she doesn't have any. I wonder why? Of course, she's never married, at least I don't think she did, so naturally there would be no children, but why didn't she ever find someone? Surely her break with Paul all those years ago wouldn't have left her that heartbroken… surely not to the point that she never fell in love again.

Mmmm… thinking of relationships, what am I going to do about Melvin? Just stop it, Gina. Don't complicate an already complicated day.

But in truth, it was all the complicated things about her life that had driven her to reach out to Jo. There had really been no time in her life for another close friend, not like Jo. Gina had shared so much of those teen and early adult years with Jo, one of the most complicated and confusing times in her life had been spent pouring out her thoughts and feelings and working through decisions with Jo. Then when her life with Robert began, Gina had no time for a new close friend. Now, here she sat several decades later with virtually no one to confide in or listen to their counsel.

How funny she thought, the counselor has no one to counsel her.

She chortled aloud in the empty room with no one to hear or find amusement in her thoughts, except herself.

Speaking of thoughts, they seemed to bounce around in her head like balls in a juggler's hand as she threw back the covers, stretched and made her way to the shower and then to dress.

She was still lost in those swirling thoughts when her cell began to ring. The screen lit up with "MARCIE" as the caller id, and she groaned. *Now what could that child possibly need this early in the morning?*

"Hi, Marcie" she said into the phone, with just a slight edge of irritation.

"Hi, Miss Gina. I'm sorry to bother you so early, but do you have time to see me this afternoon? Please, it's truly something important."

"Well, Marcie, I already have an important appointment today. Is there any way it could wait until tomorrow?"

Marcie was silent. A long, pause that said, "I really don't want to wait". After several long seconds of that silence, Gina finally relented.

"Look, I tell you what, meet me at the clinic this afternoon, around 2. If I'm a few minutes late, just wait. I will be there. Is that soon enough?"

"Yes ma'm!" an excited Marcie responded. "That will be just fine."

As Gina hung up the phone, thoughts of Marcie and the relationship they had developed momentarily overtook her thoughts.

Marcie's life had been so riddled with poverty, strife, and just plain bad luck. Gina remembered the first time they'd met…a young teenager at the clinic. Marcie was a cute, but non-descript girl in her early teens, already showing signs of resignation to a less than bright future. And, thanks to her circumstances, already participating in drug use. That's what had brought them together.

Gina had been invited to speak at the high school to bring awareness to the hidden dangers and mental health issues that were quite often a result of teen drug use. She'd so carefully prepared the speech, in hopes that something she would say might reach the ears and minds of teenagers who often felt they were ten feet tall and bullet proof. So much of what she had to say, she knew would be met with "that won't happen to me", and she knew after years as a drug counselor, that yes, of course, at some point, if they continued to use those drugs, it would happen to them.

Marcie had been on the front row. A wide-eyed, wary and somewhat pale fourteen-year-old Marcie had listened to Gina's speech, as if she were living a life built on the dangers that Gina covered in detail as she delivered her speech. Something about her face, her eyes, her dark flowing hair caught Gina's attention, and to this day she couldn't really pinpoint why. Whatever the "why" had been, Gina still felt a kind of bond with Marcie.

Even after all these years, there's so many things about Marcie's life that are a mystery to me, and apparently to her.

She'd never known her father; in fact, on her mother's deathbed she refused to tell Marcie who her father had been. Gina and Marcie had talked about every word of those last few sentences, every nuance, every possible meaning. For Marcie, it was if those sentences were pieces of a puzzle that she'd spent many years trying to solve. Every word for Marcie, held a special or hidden meaning. For Gina, some of those last few words spoke volumes about the kind of life Marcie's mother had led, and the belief that whoever fathered Marcie, was no longer alive.

Marcie hadn't really known all that much about her mother either, having lived most of her life with her grandmother. Sometime between fifteen and sixteen, Marcie's mother had returned home, only to die some six months later. She was already terminally ill when she came home to Marcie.

The child's life has been such a mess, a complete opposite to all the things I tried so hard to make sure Jax and Millie never experienced. What could she possibly want with such urgency today? Today of all days, when I don't really want or need to deal with anyone else's issues...

As she had that thought, she glanced in the mirror, sighed a disgusted sigh and turned toward the shower. As if on magical cue, her thoughts turned back to the reunion with Jo.

Now, where was I? Oh yeah, my boring-non-interesting-what-ar e-we-gonna-talk-about life?

As she stepped in the shower, she immediately chided herself for such negative thoughts, as the hot water pelted gently against her skin.

Don't be so critical of yourself. You have a lot to share with Jo. Your work has meaning. It has an impact of people's lives. And besides that, you really love what you do. How many people can make that claim?

You have Jax and Millie. Two great kids that you love to talk about.

As she thought of them, Gina's heart swelled with pride. They really were good kids. Good kids that had grown into happy, productive adults. Against all odds, especially after the loss of their dad and only a single mother to help them through adolescence.

Yes, she thought, *I can't talk about them enough. And what about those terrific grands?* Gina could imagine herself spending several hours talking about that one subject.

You need to remember that you're not supposed to do all the talking. Jorja gets to participate to, you know!

She laughed aloud at that thought.

Aw, to hell with being so worried. We were once best friends...we'll find something to talk about...

Her spirits suddenly lifted, and some of the unease evaporated, so much so that Gina burst into song as she showered and scrubbed. Scrubbing and singing her favorite Elvis tune, she managed to wash away some of the pre-dawn jitters and began to look forward to a reunion of old friends.

As she finished her shower and pulled a towel off the rack to dry, she checked herself in the mirror.

Not too shabby she thought. Her earlier disgust replaced with a laced optimism from her time in the shower. Then her thoughts returned to Jo.

The picture on Facebook Jo had posted looked so... so...what had it looked like? Not young, but not old either. Hair was perfect. Makeup non-existent. But her face looked.... sad. Like the smile she put forth didn't quite reach the heart.

I wonder if her path through life has been as complicated as mine. Does she have secrets that she keeps under lock and key? Has she ever had another friend like me? Somebody to share the weight of life's ups and downs?

Gina hadn't. She hadn't managed to ever be as close to another human being as she had been to Jo. Since neither had sisters (well, technically Jo did, but she was so much older Jo had never felt like they were sisters), they filled an emptiness for each other, that as young girls you don't even realize you have. You're just rolling through life, taking one day at a time, and never giving a second thought to the complicated adults you're about to become.

Maybe that's why today is giving me the jitters. I really miss how close we were. I really miss Jo's pragmatic look at life...her common sense advice. Life seems to be thrusting me towards a crossroads... things I must make a choice about, and I have no one to talk to about these choices.

She knew at this point in life, she truly needed a close friend. And since Jo had been that friend at such an impressionable time in her life, deep down she was putting a lot of faith in picking up the pieces of that friendship.

But is it possible to turn back time and pickup where we left off?

CHAPTER 2

7:00 am

FRESHLY SHOWERED, AND DRESSED in her best "casual, comfortable, but fit to go out in public clothes", Gina made her way to her second-best friend, the coffee pot. Ahh, the day just couldn't start without that freshly brewed, fantastically smelling, life giving pot of joe.

As she opened the cabinet to choose which strength and flavor she wanted for today, she pondered the beauty of her life.

Here I am at 54, in decent health, comfortable in my home, comfortable in my life, and lacking for none of the necessities. So why am I so in need of my old best friend?

She already knew the answer. She'd had so many conversations with herself about that very thing, that she knew the answer almost as quickly as she had the thought.

Because although on the surface everything looks so well put together and comfy, underneath I'm struggling. Struggling with my path in life. The crossroads I find myself at today, professionally and personally, aren't offering a clear way forward. My kids are grown with kids of their own. My relationship with Melvin is somewhere between halfway decent and halfway over. My time at the rehab is coming to a close… not quickly, but coming, nonetheless. Where do I go from here? How do I decide what to do with my remaining years? How do I fill up all the empty hours?

The coffee pot began to gurgle and spew, issuing forth one of her favorite flavors of the black liquid. Never one with the utmost patience, Gina began to mix the concoction she needed to partake of the perfect cup of coffee. She filled the cup with creamer, sweetener, and then lastly, she hastily removed the half-filled pot from the brewer and began to pour.

It was a delicious as she had anticipated, and with the delicious brew came more unimpeded thoughts. Thoughts and memories of a childhood and young adult life that in the same, instantaneous moment brought her a warm happiness and a twinge of regret.

Memories come sometimes with a clear timeline, a vision of yesteryear that follows a chronological timeline of events. But sometimes, memories come in jumbled, half-remembered pieces. Pieces pulled from different days, different months, different years. For Gina, the morning's memories were the jumbled bits and pieces of a lifetime of days, months and years.

Her life before the Ozarks: the many airbases, countries, people, and places of her earliest recollection of life. Germany, Japan, South Korea, her parents, her many schools, and her struggles at those schools. The dyslexia that haunted her as a child, in many ways still haunted her today. She would forever harbor a disdain for anything that required her to read from a book; not because it was that difficult today, but because she had never forgotten those feelings of frustration and incompetence as a child.

Then came the memories of her first few months in Polk Ridge. Gina had been certain that her mom and dad had moved her to the most remote, uninhabited corner of the world that they could find in her first few months as a resident of Polk Ridge. Those few months had been a lonely time for Gina, there were no beautiful Japanese gardens, no trips to Paris, no museums. Even as lonely as she felt though, she had really liked the mountains. She'd always loved hiking and had treated her new surroundings as simply another opportunity to explore and learn about everything around her.

Then she'd met Jo.

Jorja Felsenthal. She was behind the counter at the co-op, looking like she owned the place. Well, in hindsight I guess she did; at least her dad did. She was talking to somebody, with that country twang, I can still hear it now. We liked each other from the very beginning. So why should I be so worried today?

That memory led to another, then to another. Years whizzed by in Gina's mind. Her life with Robert tumbled into view.

What a happy start their dating had been. She had fallen head-over-heels for Robert from the very beginning. The giddy, knee-knocking kind of feeling that first love brings.

He was such a good man, such a good father. I still miss him today. I don't suppose I'll ever experience that kind of breathless, overwhelming attraction again. Melvin is a good guy, but I've never felt like I did with Robert.

Her mind raced again, pulling the memory of Robert's passing from a place deep within, a place she tried not to visit too often. Even today it was painful.

I'll never understand what really happened. Robert knew better, he was too focused, too aware to make a crazy mistake and put himself in danger. What was he thinking that day? What could have led him to be so reckless?

Then her mind turned to her children. The many days after Robert's accident, when she had been such a mess that even her instinct to take care of her children hadn't been forthcoming.

Bless their heart, how we survived that as well as we did, I'll never really know. They've turned into such great adults. I wish Robert could see them today. I wish he could know…

Her thoughts were interrupted by the buzzing of the phone again. This time, Gina looked forward to the conversation.

"Good morning Miss Millie."

"Good morning, Mom. Whatcha doin?"

"Drinking my coffee and thinking about you kids. What are you doin?"

Millie dodged the answer to Gina's question, with a question of her own.

"Do you ever think about anything else but us kids?"

"You didn't answer my question. But yes, I do. It just so happens that you called during my thoughts of you guys."

"Well, I'm calling cause I'm gonna need your help with the girls this afternoon, if possible. I just got a call from work, and it looks like I might be there most of the day. I've got them ready and I'm dropping them off for school, but I don't think I'll be back in time to pick them up. They get out at 2:50, do you think you could get them?"

"Mmm, I'm supposed to have an appointment at work at 2; I don't think I could get there by 2:50 but let me see if I can rearrange my appointment. If I can reschedule it to 1, then I should have plenty of time to get to the school."

"Great, just call me back. If you can't get them, I'll have to make other arrangements at work. David's guiding a bunch of tree huggers, and I can't even get in touch with him till tomorrow."

"I didn't know he was gonna be out of cell phone range. Why didn't you tell me? You know I don't like for you girls to be out there all by yourselves, I could've come to stay for a few days had I known."

"That's exactly why I didn't tell you – we're fine, and we'll be fine. I just need some help this afternoon. Call me back as soon as you know if you can work it out. OK?"

"I will. Give me about five minutes." Love you, bye."

"Love you too, Mom."

As she hung up the phone, she realized her daughter was much like herself. So independent. So headstrong. She smiled to herself. *Yes, Robert would be so very proud.*

She searched for Marcie's number on her phone. *Surely the girl could meet her at 1:00, instead of the two o'clock time they'd agreed upon.* She hit the button to dial.

"Hello…" the voice on the other end said, with some hesitation.

"Marcie, it's me, Gina. I've had something come up that I need to take care of… can we reschedule our meeting to 1:00 this afternoon, instead of 2:00?"

The voice visibly brightened.

"Oh, sure. I thought you might be calling to cancel, not reschedule. Sure, I can meet you at 1:00. I'm only working until noon, so 1:00 is even better."

In her mind's eye, Gina could see the impish grin on the other end of the line. She could see the relief that flooded Marcie's face. She knew her that well.

"Ok, great. I'll see you then. Thanks, Marcie."

"Your welcome. Bye."

Gina was still perplexed as she hung up the phone. *What did she want to talk about that was so important that it be done today?*

She refilled her coffee cup, called Millie back to let her know she could get the girls, and then sat watching the sun stream through the back-glass doors. The sunbeams it created seemed to Gina like a path…a path to a distant place, an unknown destination…or maybe that was simply how she felt about her life at the moment.

A path to a distant place…

The thought returned her to her musings of Jo and their reunion; a reunion, that as she looked at her clock, was only a matter of an hour or so away.

Oh goodness, I've got to get myself together. I need to tidy up and collect the yearbook and a few other things I wanna take with me to see Jo.

She got up from the kitchen table, poured one last cup of coffee, and went to work. Make the bed. Tidy up the bathroom. Wash up the coffee pot. All mindless work that allows for physical action, while your mind is a million miles away.

And for Gina, that meant returning to thoughts of her life.

I love this home, but it's kind of empty. It's caught somewhere between being just a house and being a real home for a family. I like living alone, I like my routine, but where am I gonna be in ten years? How am I gonna like being so alone then?

It didn't have to be this way. Melvin would have been more than willing to move in, to even marry Gina. But it wasn't what *she* wanted. She cared for Melvin; you could even call it love. But it wasn't enough; it wasn't enough for her to turn her life upside down and re-learn how to live with someone. She'd never said that to him, she'd always just dodged the issue, making some excuse every time he steered a conversation in that direction.

But what did she want from Melvin? Do I want to live with a man that always puts work first? That never has time for a family?

Melvin Kroon had never pretended to be anything other than what he was. A businessman intent on running his business successfully, and enjoying whatever time was left doing the things *he* enjoyed. Not necessarily the things a *family* would enjoy. Gina had known that from the beginning; and in the beginning, that hadn't been too much of an issue. She had been busy with kids, work, and making her own way in the world. But now, now maybe she needed to rethink the whole thing.

Now, at this point in my life, what do I really want from Melvin?

CHAPTER 3

7:30 am

AS SHE MOVED ABOUT the house, scattered in her efforts to do what little needed to be done before leaving, her thoughts remained as scattered as her activity.

Melvin was a great friend, great help when Robert died. Lord, I don't know what I would've done without him. I was a wreck and had no idea where we stood financially. Robert did all that. At best, I could balance the checkbook, but planning financially for myself, and the kids, it would've been a complete disaster without Melvin.

She remembered the day at the Krusty Kupp, the day Melvin had offered his help in any way; anything that he could do to help her, he had stood ready to do.

Yes, for all his faults, he really is a good man. A stubborn, somewhat selfish man, but nonetheless, a good man. But is that enough to base a relationship on? Memories of a good man who offered his help and then continued to be available whenever she was lonely? Or needed financial advice? Not really. It's really kind of selfish for me to have continued in the relationship, if that's all it was; a convenience for me, when it was convenient to me.

I wonder what Jo would say, if she knew the whole story. I wonder if she ever found someone and just refused to give up her career to marry? I wonder if she knows about Paul's life after she left? I wonder if she thinks of Paul, like I do Robert? I know they were never married, but they did seem to be so much in love before she left. There's so much ground for us to cover, so many missing weeks and years for us to share with each other.

Her thoughts returned to Melvin.

Well, it's not something I have to solve today. Today, I have something bigger to worry about. Melvin and I can continue to roll along just like we've been doing for the last decade, and Melvin will be just fine. Bless his heart, I do love that about him. He's content to simply move along, not really pursuing any personal objective, worried mostly about his business objective.

As she had the thought, it struck her, how in reality, she wasn't that different from Melvin.

Funny how we all have our own objectives, our own agenda, even if we're in a relationship. We still have our own path to follow. Maybe Melvin wasn't willing to compromise in certain areas of his life, but then, for the most of their relationship, neither had she.

Gina was so lost in her thoughts, that the sound of the doorbell chiming made her jump and utter a loud gasp.

Dammit. I don't have time for somebody at my door this morning. Who in the hell could be here this early?

"Coming!" she shouted from the bedroom. Hoping she hadn't voiced her thoughts aloud.

As she opened the door, the man of her thoughts stood before her, soaked in something red.

"Melvin, what on earth? What's all over your shirt? What are you doin here so early this morning? Why aren't you at work?"

"You know, that's what I love about you Gina. You can ask more questions in two seconds than any human being can possibly answer in fifteen minutes."

She could tell by his tone that he was a little more than disgruntled and didn't appreciate her round of questions in the least.

"Well, start with the first one – what is that on your shirt?"

"It's tomato sauce."

"Ok, so how did you get tomato sauce all over you, and does that really warrant a trip to see me?"

"It does. I got this all over me because one of the waitresses at work managed to spill a whole can, and I just happened to be in the line of fire. I don't have another shirt at work, but I thought maybe you had one of mine here. And, your place is closer than mine. So, do you think I could come in, or you just want me to stand out here like a big red tomato while we discuss the situation?"

"Oh, oh yes, come on in. And yes, I've got one of your work shirts here; remember, you asked me to mend the pocket a couple of weeks ago. It's clean and hanging in the laundry room."

Gina opened the door wide, made room for him to come inside, then went to fetch the shirt.

Gina's thoughts were suddenly overtly sarcastic. *Of course, he would come here. Of course, Gina always has the solution when it comes to shirts, pants, and mending. Of course, that's all that Melvin really needs Miss Gina to do; take care of the domestic issues.*

She was instantly sorry for her thoughts, but it didn't change the fact that for the most part, that's exactly how she felt about Melvin's thoughts of her.

"Here, here's the clean shirt, go to the bathroom and change, and then bring me the tomato-sauce shirt. That stain can't sit, or it will never come out."

"Yes ma'am. Just as you say ma'am. I'll be right back ma'am."

Melvin's tone was more than a little sarcastic as he headed for the bathroom.

Maybe we're both way past this relationship. Maybe we're both just reluctant to admit it.

"What's got you in such a tizzy this morning?" Melvin shouted from the bathroom. "I thought you'd be taking it easy, drinking coffee and contemplating how to spend your day."

"Of course, you've forgotten what today is, haven't you?" Gina shouted back to the bathroom.

Of course, he had. It didn't have anything to do with him, or the Krusty Kupp so he simply tossed it out of his head.

"What're you talking about? What is today? It's not your birthday, it's not…" his voice trailed off, as he pulled the clean shirt over his head.

"I'm supposed to see Jorja today. Remember? I'm supposed to be at her house at 8:30, and your visit isn't helping me keep my schedule. Are you almost finished?"

"Oh, yeah. I did forget about that. Yes, here… here's the dirty shirt." He handed if off to her as he walked past. "Well, I'm not here to mess up your schedule. I gotta get back to work ASAP. It's busy this morning, and if that shirt hadn't been such a total mess, I wouldn't have left at all."

He gave her a swift peck on the check, and out the door he went.

Just like that. Get the clean shirt, leave the dirty shirt. See ya later, Gina.

She took the tomato sauce covered shirt to the laundry room and took out her feelings of frustration on the shirt and the shout she poured over the stain in an effort to remove as much as possible before tossing it in the wash.

Now I'm either not gonna get all my stuff done, or I'm gonna be late. To hell with it. I don't care if it hair lips the Pope, I'm not gonna be late to see Jo.

She glanced at the clock again, as she came out of the laundry room. Less than thirty minutes before she would be pulling up at Jo's cabin. Only about fifteen before she had to leave. *Dammit.*

CHAPTER 4

8:00 am

SHE FLEW THROUGH THE rest of the housework, giving most everything nothing more than a lick and a promise.

This stuff can be done right later today. I just need to hit the high spots.

Already her morning and her plans had been invaded by those she held dearest and as was often the case, she had rearranged her life to meet those demands.

The hazards of motherhood and being in a relationship. I don't know why I'm irritated, I can't imagine what life would be like without all these interruptions.

And with that thought, Jo invaded her mind once again.

She has no children. She has no husband, maybe a relationship with someone, but no husband; and if judging by her last name is any indication, she's either never had one, or didn't think much of him. She's still Jo Felsenthal on her Facebook page, anyway. You know, this is sad. This woman was my best friend when we were kids, but you could put what I know about her now in a thimble. Well, seeing her today will probably go one of two ways, with probably no middle ground. We'll either pickup where we left off, or we'll have very, very, little to share.

Stopped with that thought and stood before the mantle in her living room. There, placed with love and care, side by side on the shelf, were pictures of the people she loved and couldn't imagine her life without. Jax, Millie, the twins, even a picture of she and Melvin resided to one end of the display. Replacing the picture of she and Robert with one of her and Melvin had been one of the hardest things Gina had ever done. It was such a simple act, but it had taken every ounce of her resolve to make the switch.

The one picture she had never replaced was a photo of she and Jo, taken when they were about fifteen or sixteen. They had decided that day to hike in the mountains behind Jo's house. They both shared a deep love of those mountains, and all the beauty they held when viewed from the side of a cliff or at the very top. The sights of that day were as clear in Gina's mind as if she had only seen them yesterday.

That day had been such a wonderful day. They'd packed a lunch and a few snacks into a couple of backpacks and started early, just as the sun peeked over the treetops in Jo's backyard.

We were so full of life. So free, so naïve. We thought the world was ours to conquer. All those plans about the places we wanted to go, the people we wanted to meet. The things we wanted to do with our lives. If I remember right, it was the summer before our junior year. How could we have possibly known the roads we were about to take would be so very different from the ones we were planning?

It was with a wistful, almost sorrowful expression that Gina finally turned away from the photos and finished her work.

Life is such a crazy place. Such a myriad of choices, paths, and un-intended consequences.

As she walked by the microwave, she once again checked the clock. 8:10am.

Shit, I've got to get my stuff together and get outta here. I'll never make it by 8:30 if I don't stop and go on.

She went once more to the bathroom mirror.

That's as good as it's gonna get. No movie star, but hair and my little bit of makeup look ok.

She slipped on her favorite pair of sneakers and was as ready as she would ever be.

I'm still a little uneasy. Maybe we should've decided to meet at the Krusty Kupp. At least there, we'd have other distractions if we can't keep a conversation going just between us.

If I'd have set it up there, Melvin could help with the conversation. He's never at a loss for words. In fact, I believe he probably defies all the odds about women talking more than men.

Why I am having such a ridiculous line of thoughts? Just stop. Just get moving.

CHAPTER 5

GINA GATHERED HER PURSE, keys, and phone. It was time. She went out the kitchen door, closed and locked it, and got in the car.

Will she be excited to see me? Will the years roll away? Damn! I forgot the yearbook. Ah, just go back and get it. If things aren't the same between you two, at least you'll have something to look at and talk about.

After retrieving the yearbook, she started the car and backed out of the driveway. Jo's cabin was only a short distance, but it seemed almost an eternity to Gina. Twenty minutes later, she turned down her drive.

Gina could still recall Jo's smile as she left Little Rock. Leaving her behind. Not because she wanted to, but because she had to.

She had to leave, and I had to stay, Gina reminded herself.

So much time had passed. Now, she longed for the closeness she once had with her best friend. Could they recapture and rekindle their friendship?

Even the beautiful April morning, sunshine and Elvis on the radio couldn't calm Gina's nerves.

I'm here. I'm really here, she thought. *And I'm really nervous. It's been so many years. For the thousandth time, she asked herself, "Will we have anything in common now?"*

Had time and different lives robbed them of that great bond, or would it be as simple and comforting as putting on an old sweater. Could it, would it, be that easy to reconnect?

Gina's sneakers made no sound as she moved from her car to the front door. All she heard was the thud of her heart. Excitement and dread filled her simultaneously. Would the years roll away with the opening of the front door? A sinking feeling of apprehension made her want to turn and run, but her need to fill the void of closeness and familiarity with her old friend steadied her gait toward the front door. Whatever the outcome, the moment of truth was at hand.

She rang the bell.

CHAPTER 6

Wednesday, May 19th, 2012, Jo Remembers....
5:30 am

JO'S ALARM BEEPED AT 5:30am. She stretched a slender, floppy, sleepy hand from beneath the covers and hit the snooze button. The night had been long and filled with endless dreams of nonsensical bits and pieces of ancient people and places she rarely gave a waking conscious thought to.

As she lay in that drowsy, half-conscious place between dreaming and waking reality, she recalled the airport, the goodbyes, and a brief feeling of excitement coursed through sleepy veins. In her dream state, when she turned from waving her goodbyes, it was to face a demon in the form of a cadet, an upper-class cadet whose name and face was forever emblazoned in Jo's mind. The affect of seeing that face again, even in a dream was jolting. Her eyes flew open wide. Dreaming and excitement replaced by loathing, the warmth of the airport goodbye, replaced by the feel of ice water in her veins.

Not today. Not dealing with that today, she thought as she threw the covers wide.

Time to get up and get moving. There's a lot of ground to cover this morning before Gina gets here, and thoughts of THAT aren't part of the plan.

Jo slid from the covers, made a pit stop in the bathroom, and padded to the kitchen. *Coffee, must have coffee.*

She absolutely loved the new Keurig that she'd purchased once back in Polk Ridge. She'd never even given it a thought in D.C., continuing to use the same old Mr. Coffee she'd had for years. But packing it up to move had resulted in a broken glass decanter, and the end of the Mr. Coffee.

She opened the cabinet doors to survey her flavor choices for the morning and decided on a Columbian dark roast. Perfect choice to bring her sleepy mind to life.

She popped it in the holder, slid her favorite cup under the dispenser, and chose the strong option. As the coffee began to flow, she looked out her kitchen window.

It's going to be a beautiful day. Not a cloud in the sky, slight breeze, birds are already chirping. What a gorgeous view of the mountains I'll have as the sun comes up...

She grabbed her coffee, the pack of Marlboro lights she'd left on the bar, and went out the back sliding glass doors.

The cabin Jo had rented sat nestled on the side of one of the smaller hills that belonged to the Ozark Mountain chain. They had been built far enough from people and each other to feel remote, without actually being remote. In fact, they were spaced close enough, that she could see smoke rising from another cabin in the not so distant valley below.

Why in the world had Paul Collections decided to build these cabins? I would've figured he had his hands full with the winery. I need to do a little digging when Gina gets here and catchup on exactly how Mr. Collections has been spending his time and what he's done with his parents' winery. I wonder if he still has it?

She plopped into one of the oversized patio chairs, lit a cigarette, inhaled deeply then exhaled, blowing smoke that formed a cloud of blue around her head and took a sip of the strong coffee. *Perfect morning.*

She allowed her thoughts to wander on the memories of Paul Collections, her choice to leave, and what might have been, had she chosen to stay.

No sense walking down a path that was never meant for you to travel, Missy, she chided herself. *You were never going to be satisfied spending your life in Polk Ridge. And you were never going to be satisfied working in a family winery..*

Her thoughts switched suddenly to Gina.

She left herself no other choice...she's had to be satisfied here and figure out how to make a life in a place that's lost in time.

With the thought of time, Jo realized the sun was peaking ever so coquettishly over the tip of the mountain directly in front of her. The colors that pierced the morning sky were hues of purples, pinks, reds, and oranges. *This place may be lost in time, but it's a beautiful way to be lost...*

She took another sip of the aromatic coffee, finished her cigarette and sat simply enjoying the beauty that lay sprawling in front of her. *I had forgotten how beautiful it is here. I've been so busy looking at the world view from 30,000 feet, I forgot how to enjoy the simplicity of my own backyard view.*

She spent the next twenty minutes reflecting on her life, the choices she'd made and how even the most worldly of paths can take such unexpected turns.

It was with some reluctance that she pulled herself out of her reverie, went for another cup of coffee and headed on to the bathroom for a quick shower.

CHAPTER 7

JO STOPPED BY HER closet on the way to shower, chose one of her favorite "casual but chic" outfits, and took a quick look in the mirror.

Well, not too shabby. A few wrinkles here and there, but not too bad for 53.

Then she stopped to notice the many changes that had been occurring with her body as she began to age.

Saggy here, droopy there, flabby in more places than I care to count. You would think after all those years of PT, I'd still be as fit as a fiddle. I've had too many years at a desk, and not enough time in the field.

Time in the field…who could have imagined the journey I started as a kid, would take me to all the places I've been? To all the different posts I've held, never mind my work at the Dept of Defense. Hell, I'd never even heard of the internet when I enlisted. Life has held some really big surprises for me…some good, some bad.

She threw her pajamas over the hook on the bathroom door, and stepped into a hot, steamy shower.

The water seemed to wash away some of her melancholy mood, and when she emerged, the body that had just a few moments ago seemed so distasteful, glowed pink and a smile touched Jo's lips.

I may be a little worse for the wear, but I'm not completely out of the game. But am I even interested in pursuing a relationship? Now, at my age, do I really want to put all that effort into something that, in the end, may or may not work?

Paul Collections and Phillip Smart wandered into her thoughts.

Those two are the only ones to have ever held my heart. Yet they're so different. What is it about a person that touches a heart? What was it about either of them that caught my attention? And how did I let them both slip away?

She already knew the obvious answer to the question. She had chosen herself and her career over any feelings of romance and love that either man had brought into her life. *But why did I chose myself over them? Why wasn't I able to take a leap of faith and give up some of what I wanted in order to gain what "we" might have been?*

It was a question she had ask herself a million times over. And the truth was, she still hadn't come up with an answer that was satisfying.

She wasn't raised in a selfish home. Her mother and father had given to each other selflessly in a marriage that for all appearances had been a happy one. She had never been a spoiled, selfish child. Yes, her Dad had gone above and beyond to make sure Jo had most of what she wanted, and all of what she needed.

I can hear him now,"Jo, you have a lot to be thankful for, just look around. There are lots of kids who would like to walk in your shoes."

The only thing I can say for sure, is that I always wanted to do something with my life. Something more than be a wife and mother. I wanted something…something just for me…a life that has been lived, just for me.

Perhaps it had been those early years of watching Stella and Jack. Watching as Stella gave up so much of herself to become "Jack's wife", that had left an indelible print on Jo's subconscious. Stella was so much older than Jo, that at times it had seemed as though she had no sister at all. Maybe two mothers, but not a sister. Watching as a ten-year old, Jo had developed feelings of animosity toward Jack. Feelings she had never really reconciled, and that only seemed to get worse after she returned home. The more she talked to her mom and Stella, the more she learned about Jack and his love of scotch.

I really need to call Stella. The last time we talked, something was just a little off with her. I'm not sure if it's the boys, or Jack, or just Stella and her moods. But something just isn't quite right…

She glanced at the clock, only 6:15.

Good job. You've got plenty of time to finish before Gina arrives.

She moved through the rest of her morning dressing routine. Towel dry the hair, light dusting of perfume, blow dry her hair, and pull on her clothes.

She surveyed the finished product in the mirror.

Good enough. You'll never be eighteen again, and you're never gonna look like it. Just work with what ya got, Jo.

As she began to straighten the bathroom, her thoughts returned to the two men she'd loved and lost.

They were entirely different people. Yet both captured my heart. Maybe if Paul had come along at a different time in my life, maybe it would have been different. Maybe I would have been more settled, more confident in who I was and I could've found a way to fit into Paul's life. I really did love him, maybe it was just that teenage first love kind of thing, but it was real.

The thought of his life, lived without her, and as far as she knew, completely absorbed by his family's winery, brought her back around to the cabins he now owned.

Maybe I didn't see in Paul at eighteen, what I should have seen. He's apparently done quite well for himself, and maybe our lives would have been more than… more than what? More than simply existing in Polk Ridge? Wasn't that the fear that had prevented her from making a life with him?

She shook the thoughts of Paul, only to see Phillip Smart as they'd parted that day in Japan.

Now there was a relationship that had been beyond weird. Everything was so hurried, I never expected it to be over so soon. Our time together, the chance we had to grow and be in love after falling in love wasn't enough. We were supposed to have another year. Maybe if I'd told Phillip how I felt, maybe we could have made the long distance thing work. Or maybe not…I don't think Phillip was ever as in love with me as I was with him. But the ending of everything was just so strange. One day he's there, and the next he's not. Literally, he wasn't there physically, emotionally, nothing. It was like he turned off a faucet.

Those thoughts brought her back around to thinking of the two men and comparing the situations.

Paul loved me deeply, and I wasn't ready. I loved Phillip, and he wasn't ready. Life is such a crazy place. It's hard sometimes to look at things from both sides of the coin, but that's exactly what those two provided for me… a chance to see both sides.

She finished in the bathroom and made her way to the living room, which at the moment doubled as her office and classroom.

Time to take a look at work and class material, not think about your love life.

CHAPTER 8

6:30 am

JO SAT DOWN AND pressed the start button on her laptop. There'd been no need to ask for the usual travel setup. A desktop computer with all the trimmings simply wasn't necessary anymore. The equipment the DOD had sent to secure her connection wasn't nearly as elaborate as the setup she'd had in D.C., but just as functional and consumed a lot less space. And, space was something she was just a little short of.

We have come a long way…

As she went through the motions of starting the system, logging in to her email accounts, and beginning her morning routine of checking for updates from students and coworkers alike, she thought about those early years. She clearly remembered the day her career path began, and realized so many of her life's choices had been cemented in those few moments.

That meeting in the dean's office was monumental. It was the beginning of so many opportunities, so many choices that would shape my life. I still sometimes have trouble believing what they offered me…I was so unprepared for that day.

As Jo had entered her fourth class cadet year at the academy, technology change for the military was moving at much the same speed Jo's life was changing. The internet was in its infancy, but already the military was charging forward, making the most of the open door that global access offered in the way of intelligence gathering and spying.

Her degree in engineering had opened the door. But during her fourth year, a new component had been added: computers, internet, and the development of information sharing systems. When Jo finished her time there, she had a long list of accomplishments, and a degree in a brand new field: Computer Engineering.

Funny how when you're in the midst of something, you don't really realize the magnitude and the impact that "something" may have on the world around you. I would never have dreamed the things we were working on and developing would have produced what we have today.

Now, years later, those same skills were still opening doors for her.

Jo was still lost in thought when she heard the familiar buzz of her cell phone. "Maggie" appeared on the dark screen.

"Good morning, my friend. How are things on your side of the world?" Jo's voice was as warm as the morning sun that filtered across her living room. She was, it seemed looking forward to a visit from Gina, and that happy anticipation bled over into the tone of her voice.

"Good morning, my remote mountain friend. You seem to be in a really good mood. Everything's just peachy here, not that you really want me to elaborate on all the "peachy" events in detail. How are you over there in hermit land?"

"It's not hermit land, Maggie. There are plenty of people to see and things to do, it's just not as easily accomplished as it is there. You'll be interested to know I do have something planned with another actual living person today. Gina's coming over."

"Oh. Now remind me again, what's her story? You two were best friends once, right?"

"Yes, that's right. Gina and I basically grew up together. We just went in completely different directions when we graduated high school, and I did a really poor job of keeping in touch. Well, actually we both did."

"She's the one that stayed up there in that godforsaken, no-internet-access, mountain world, right?

Jo sighed. Maggie was so direct.

"Yes, she stayed here for all of her life, so far as I know. I'll have more to share about her after visit today. Now, what did you call for? I know it wasn't to simply disparage my mountain roots."

Maggie laughed, and as she did, her own country upbringing was more pronounced. She had a low, throaty, full laugh; and one that was highly contagious.

"No, that's not why I called. I've got something happening in one of the chat rooms I've been monitoring, and I need your input to decode some of the messages."

"Can you email it to me? I'm really trying to get my ducks in a row before Gina gets here this morning, and I don't have time for a lengthy conversation."

"Sure. Although I really wanted to talk through this with you.." Maggie's voice trailed.

She's hoping I'll change my mind and spend the next half hour working on this.

"I know you did, but I really don't have time first thing this morning. Can you give me till early afternoon?"

"Yeah, I'll just email it to you. But let me know something as soon as you can. I really do need this as soon as you can work on it."

"I will. Gina's coming around 8:30, and as soon as the visit is over, I'll get to work on this."

"8:30? Why so dang early? I don't like visitors till afternoon."

"Well, some of us actually enjoy getting up early and starting the day. Besides, it was Gina's suggestion, not mine."

They talked on for a another few minutes, and then Jo insisted that she needed to go. Maggie was never at a loss for words, and never minded engaging another as long as they would participate.

As she hung up the phone, she thought about her friendship with Maggie, and all the years they had known each other.

Maggie Wilson, aka Margaret Ann Wilson, had been one of her fellow female cadets all those many years ago. Maggie was then, and still to this day, a true friend. Different than her friendship with Gina had been, but nonetheless, a true friend.

Maggie didn't want to participate in your problems. Maggie didn't want to know that much about your personal life. She was always more focused on where your career and work life was going. Some would say that was just a little shallow, but Jo knew it wasn't. Jo knew that was just Maggie. She didn't like to talk about her personal issues, and she didn't want you to talk about yours.

Ah, Maggie. Such a colorful combination of character conflicts. They'll never make another one of her.

Maybe that had more to do with their field training and Jack Valley than Jo or Maggie would ever admit.

Maggie had in reality shared one of the most horrific events of Jo's life. It had been Maggie that came to her immediately after, and Maggie that had talked her through the tears, the pain, and the disbelief. It had been Maggie that had finally helped her to cope and find her way back from the urge to run, and keep running. It had been Maggie that Jo had leaned on to find the mental strength to bury the events of that night and move on with her life.

Jack Valley had scarred them both. Maybe that's why Maggie had developed the wall she carried with her now. Maybe helping Jo deal with the pain of the night's events had taken all that Maggie had to give. It had taken almost everything Jo had had to give for a very long time.

But I'm not going to think about all that today. Not that…I just can't revisit that today. Thank God for Maggie that night. Thank God for Maggie in the weeks that followed. But that's enough of that. Now, where was I…

She returned to the computer and tasks at hand. Checking class schedules, correspondence from her students, and any emails from her coworkers in D.C.

As she clicked through the class information, she was glad she had signed up to teach.

You know, working with these students, puts life in a completely different perspective. Rather than being concerned with only the things happening in my life, they've given me a chance to share my knowledge, and watch as that knowledge makes an impact on their lives. It's really a rewarding thing.

It took her only a few minutes to pick out the emails that needed an immediate response, and she put the rest of them on follow up for later in the day.

I've got to spend some time looking at tomorrow's class topic, and make sure I have everything in order…we're getting close to test time, and I want my students to be as prepared as possible… they may not realize it, but this material is going to be so very important for them.

Once again, her thoughts were interrupted by the buzzing of the phone.

What now…

She glanced at the phone, half expecting it to say "George" or "Maggie", but her aggravation was short lived when she saw that it was her mom on the other end of the line.

Mmmm… this is unusual.

CHAPTER 9

7:00 am

"HEY, MOM. YOU'RE AN early bird today."

"Yes, I guess I am. But I needed to see if you could come over today."

Jo still wasn't accustomed to change in Maureen's voice. The voice that had always been on the other end, had for all of Jo's life been one of quiet assurance. A steady, rhythmic, confident, assuring tone. Now, it seemed to Jo, all at once, that voice was gone; replaced by one of less strength, more unsure, and downright disconcerting for her daughter.

"Sure, I can come over, but it'll be later on this afternoon. Is that soon enough?"

"Yes, I got some things in the mail from the hospital yesterday, and I'm not sure what I need to do. Some of them are bills, but they're so confusing. And some of the stuff, I really don't know what I'm supposed to do. It looks like appointments, or something. I wanted you to take a look."

"Ok. I'll be over around 3. Just don't worry about the mail, we'll look at it together and figure out what we need to do. Did you have a good night, last night?"

"No, I didn't, Jo. I just tossed and turned. I couldn't ever get really comfortable. That bed of mine is just worn out. I think I need a new mattress. That's something else we can talk about today too."

"Yes, we can talk about that too. Just don't worry about stuff like that. That's one of the reasons I came home. I need to be here to help you, even if the problem is only a bed mattress. I'll be over at 3. You remember Gina's coming to visit today, right?"

"Oh, no. I had forgotten. Ok, just go ahead and get yourself ready. We'll look at all my stuff this afternoon. Love you honey, bye."

"Love you too, Mom. See ya later today."

Jo ended the call and sat for several minutes, uncomfortable dread consuming her body and mind.

I know she's not well. I know something more than a broken leg is wrong with Mom. I also know this will be different than losing Dad. This time with Mom, no matter how long or short, will require much more from me than when Dad passed. I'm just not ready to lose another parent. I'm not ready to feel so alone again.

Jo remembered all too clearly the weeks and months that had followed Tom Felsenthal's passing. Her life had been so busy, she had been so consumed with her career; yet even that couldn't hold at bay the loneliness she felt after losing her Dad. He had been her rock. Her Dad. Her friend. Her confidant. And then he was gone.

She had been in Japan, involved in one of the many projects she had been assigned, when she got the call. She didn't think she was going to make it home in time. She'd had so many emotional, heart-breaking moments on the plane home. So many memories of her days at the co-op with her Dad. So many memories.

She had barely gotten to the hospital; her only time with her Dad had been ten short minutes. Ten minutes to say so much to the man who had been such a huge part of her life. Ten minutes to say how much she loved him, and then goodbye.

Ten minutes. That's all I had with Dad. Just ten minutes. Lord, please give me more time with Mom. Please give me plenty of days to take care of her, share with her, and say a really long goodbye.

Jo, by choice, had never been a caregiver. She'd never had children, her father's death had been so quick it wasn't necessary, and she hadn't been around when her grandparents were in need of help. Taking care of someone, other than herself, was a new role for Jo. One she had hoped she could handle just as she had handled a career.

Taking care of Mom isn't going to be like scheduling meetings and looking at daily appointments on a calendar. I can see already, this role in my life is going to be more like a rollercoaster ride. Unexpected issues, unexpected visits, unexpected opportunities to make a few more memories. This is going to be hard. Gina. Gina knows what some of this is like. Especially since she has worked with and counselled so many people. I'll talk to her about what to expect. What it might be like. She's taking care of her Dad too, I think.

With the thought of Gina, came the realization that she needed to check the time. Jo still had plenty to do before she was ready for a visit with Gina.

7:15. I've still got plenty of time to finish checking my emails from Maggie and George, and anybody else with a problem, before I get up to finish tidying up.

Jo spent the next ten minutes or so answering the emails that only required a short, uninvolved response. Yes to this. No to that. I'll look at that today for you.

She flew through most of her correspondence in those few minutes, and then went back to reviewing her notes for tomorrow's class.

Jo had returned to school in 2005 to get a teaching degree. With the computer engineering degree she already held, it took only a couple of years to get the remaining classes complete, and suddenly, she was a teacher. She had still needed to pass state boards for the state of Nevada, but now that she had completed that exam, she was a fully, licensed, teacher of Computer Science. Amazingly, Jo truly enjoyed what she was doing. She had never really thought of herself as teacher material, but her students seemed to really enjoy her classes, and she was becoming increasingly comfortable with her role.

These online classes are pretty cool. I like the fact that I don't have to show up on a college campus every day, or sit in a stuffy class room. Teaching in this environment, allows me to be close to Mom, comfortable at home, and really enjoy sharing with these kids. Who would've thought all those years ago, the work we were doing in the military, would have so many real world applications. Like online classes, emails, shopping, spying, surveillance; my God, the list is staggering and quit thinking about work.

She glanced at her clock again. 7:29am.

I gotta get up and get busy.

CHAPTER 10

7:30 am

THE CABIN JO HAD chosen from the list that Paul sent was one of the smaller ones. She had known she wouldn't need one of the larger ones, and it really wasn't fair to take one, especially since Paul had offered the use of any one she wanted, free of charge.

Cabin X, as it was officially labeled on the post positioned at the beginning of the rather long and winding drive was a two bedroom, one bath log cabin. The logs were real logs, and formed the exterior, as well as the interior of the cabins living room and kitchen area. Both bedrooms and bath included interior walls of sheet rock; necessary for the installation of fixtures, plugs, and water lines. Cabinets in the kitchen hid the necessary plumbing and piping for all the kitchen fixtures, but left little opportunity for wall accessories.

This fact, however, bothered Jo very little. Not one to need or want an excessive amount of personal décor, she had found herself right at home from day one.

She had hired a moving company to bring all her things from D.C., and had only arrived one day prior to receiving their email that the truck would deliver on the following Monday. That left her only the weekend to survey her cabin, figure out where to put everything and direct them when they arrived. She had spent her first weekend at her mom's, but the following week had been filled with making the cabin her temporary home.

The cabin itself was positioned on the side of a hill; a hill, that it seemed to Jo had been put there just for the building of a small, one-person dwelling.

Large glass windows formed one end of the expansive living room area, and afforded any occupant with a view of the surrounding mountains and the valley below. Over the last several weeks, Jo had found herself mesmerized by this view, and completely lost in thought, rather than focused on the work at hand.

It was no different this morning. As she moved about the small cabin, straightening this, moving that, and making her small area seem more organized with each effort, she couldn't help but glance out the windows and admire the scenery before her.

I guess if you have to move back home, this is one of the best ways to do it. Gorgeous views, comfortable living areas, and as close to mom as I could have ever hoped to be. Thank you, Paul for this. I suppose I need to send him some sort of "thank you" memento. I could never have hoped to be so settled and comfortable without his help.

Funny, when I thought about moving home, I never thought the people I had left behind would be so much help, or be so willing to be a help. Life is such a crazy, weird thing.

Her thoughts consumed her mind, while picking up and cleaning up consumed her physical being. It wasn't like there was that much to do, after all, Jo was still as much a military being as she was a female. Years and years of military life had instilled in her the need for an organized life, and this carried down to her personal living as well.

Everything has a place, everything in its place. I realize I'm a little OCD about my lifestyle, but what the hell, it's only me. It's only me...

That simple, single phrase brought her to an abrupt halt, right in the middle of fluffing a cushion on one of her living room chairs.

It's only me. All these years, all the people I've met, all the places I've been, and it all comes to down to "it's only me". No kids, no husband,

and no really close friends. Sure there's George and Maggie, but they're hundreds of miles away, and still so involved in their work. These last few weeks haven't been that bad, but I've been so busy setting up house, of course it wouldn't be too bad. But what about the next few weeks? What about the next few months? Sure I've got Mom to see about, and I'm sure that will take up a lot of my time. But Mom's not capable of being a confidant, a "let's-go-somewhere-and-do-something" kind of relationship. Hell, she needs care, not carefree, spur of the moment trips.

The evenings George, Maggie and myself spent talking shop, eating out and enjoying each other – how will I find that here? Who can I find that with here? I mean, I'm looking forward to visiting with Gina, but do she and I still have anything in common? I bet I sure as hell can't talk work with her. She has no idea the kind of intelligence and classified information I work with….I used to work with.

With that thought, she revisited her decision to come home, and the choices she'd had to make about work.

Maureen's accident had been the catalyst that finally pushed Jo to do more than think about giving up her work and returning home. She'd finally realized going home was something she was going to have to do more than think about.

Her teaching degree had been a godsend. Several years prior, Jo had decided to return to school to get the degree, and now, as she stood at a career crossroads, she was more than thankful. Having teaching to fall back on, had made it somewhat easier to make the break from her work in D.C.

But have I really made a break from work? Maggie and George still call like it's my job to help them. The Department sent "the black box" with me, just like I would need secure access for work…

She smiled to herself. *Maybe I'm the only one that thinks I turned in my notice and no longer work at the department.*

Quite wallowing in self-pity. Sure, you now find yourself somewhat alone, but you're not really all alone. George and Maggie are coming out to visit in the fall. Gina's coming over to visit you today.

Oooh…Gina's coming, get it in gear. Quit wasting time thinking about poor little Jo's solitary life…

She glanced at the clock. Five til 8.

Hurry up, chic. You wanna have time for one more cup of coffee and cigarette before Gina gets here.

CHAPTER 11

JO STRODE OVER THE kitchen and placed her cup under the Keurig dispenser once more.

This time she chose a lighter blend, the dark roast had done its job. Now she wanted something light and aromatic to sit down with.

One more cup and one more cigarette, then it will probably be time for Gina.

Jo had spent several hours the day before looking for her high school yearbook. She'd gone through every still unpacked box and hadn't managed to locate the yearbook. In fact, she hadn't managed to locate any of her high school stuff. No diploma, no yearbook, no graduation invitations.

Now as she sat enjoying the last few moments of solitude for the morning, she wondered what she'd done with all those mementos.

Maybe I left them at Mom's a few years ago. I know I sent some boxes to her before I made my move to D.C. Maybe all that stuff was in a couple of those boxes. Oh, and yeah, I know I stored some of the stuff the moving company brought. I bet that's where it is.

I would like to have that yearbook this morning. It would help, if we can't find that much to talk about.

Thoughts of the yearbook stirred old memories. Old memories that seemed like a whole other lifetime; in fact, a whole different person's life.

Her mind returned to memories of a lifetime ago..

The old iron bridge...fall of 1975...that's where we four made so many memories...

The old iron bridge was THE place to be when Jo and Gina were teenagers. Every Friday night after a ballgame, every spring break, every summer weekend, every body wanted to hang out, and the bridge was the place they all picked.

Jo, Gina, Robert and Paul had spent more nights just hanging out around a beach fire that someone had decided to build, than they could recount.

It was here that so many teenage dreams had been shared. So many stunts and pranks planned. So many happy times for the four of them.

I remember so clearly the last time we were there and the afternoon he invited here there...

Jo had been on her way to the library when Paul stopped her in the hall. They were in a battle for the title of class Valedictorian. And it was turning out to be a real battle.

"Jo, hey Jo. Hold up a minute."

"What? I gotta get to the library before the bell rings."

"You know we're tied right now for the spot, right?"

"What spot?"

"You know what spot."

She grinned at him across the hall. A big, wide, innocent grin.

"Yeah, but we still got to the end of the year to go, and I will win, Paul. You just wait and see."

"You really want this, don't you?"

"Of course I do, but I wanna win it fair and square. It's no good if you don't give it your best shot, you understand me? I don't wanna win cause you want me to. I wanna win because I did better than you."

"I'm not gonna let you win, because if you do, I'll never live it down. I can hear my ol' man saying 'Paul, I can't believe you let some girl beat you.' Oh no, I'm not gonna listen to that."

"You might have to, especially if you don't pull that chemistry grade up past an 88. Mine's 92 – gotcha beat so far."

"I got time. But what I don't have time to do is talk to you right now. What you doin' after the annual staff meeting?"

"Not much. Gotta run by the co-op and then go home. Why?"

"Meet me at the bridge around 5pm. We really need to talk before graduation."

"Graduation? Now? Why?"

He gave her a look that said *Not here, not now.*

"Okay", she relented. "See ya then."

A smiled touched her lips as she recalled the day. *I couldn't figure it out then. But it was extremely clear just a few short hours later.*

I suppose I remember so much about that day because I was so confused about why he couldn't talk to me right there. We were standing right there in the hall, with nothing but air and opportunity between us. Looking back, I should've suspected something more than idle chatter.

She'd gotten to the bridge just a few minutes after five, and no Paul in sight.

Jo had killed the first fifteen minutes skipping rocks across the water. Then she'd began to lose patience and at 5:25 was getting in her car to go home.

I can only imagine how he must have felt when he drove up, and I was such a jerk. I had no idea…

"Where have you been? I thought you said 5?"

"I'm sorry, I did say 5, but dad wouldn't let me leave the counter 'til 5, so that's why I'm late. Thank you for waiting."

"It's alright. I needed a few minutes to myself anyway. What did you wanna talk about graduation for? It's still months away."

"It's not really graduation I wanted to talk to you about." He paused for a moment. "Jo, we've been dating for a while now, and I've known you most of my life, and…I need to tell you something."

"Well, if it's about the Valedictorian thing," Jo interrupted, "It doesn't matter about us dating. It's not gonna change anything between us."

"No, listen. It's not that. We have so much in common. You love learning as much as I do, and you're so smart and funny, and you're almost the prettiest girl I've ever seen, but…"

Jo had interrupted him again. "I thought I *was* the prettiest girl you'd ever seen, she laughed. "C'mon, Paul, what are you trying to say? You tired of datin' me?"

"No! I'm trying to tell you I love you…

Just as quickly as he had spit the words out, he stopped. His face turning a bright, crimson color, then almost as quickly, a paleness replaced the crimson.

"Ever since I kissed you, I've been falling in love with you. I know you want to leave Polk Ridge and do something with your life. But we could do so much here. You could do so much with me. I just want you to know how I feel and ask if you feel the same way. I need to know you'll be a part of my life, even after we graduate."

Jo had watched his heart break, as hers was breaking for him. She couldn't tell him she loved him. Although in hindsight, she was sure she did. She was as sure of that as she was sure that she had been going to leave.

And for that reason, she had withheld from him how she truly felt.

I was leaving, no matter what, and he had to stay no matter what.

When Jo had finished explaining why they could never be, why she couldn't stay, his face had looked defeated. His eyes brimmed with unshed tears.

His voice had been pleading.

"I can wait, Jo. I can wait 'til you see what you gotta see, if you'll just tell me you'll come back. I can wait for you."

Jo was smoking her third cigarette, and the coffee had grown cold when she snapped out of her reverie.

Another lifetime, another person ago. I don't know if coming home is worth all of this reflection. Some of these memories still pull at my heart…

She crushed the cigarette, pickup up the coffee and headed inside.

On second thought, me and Gina have a lot to talk about…

CHAPTER 12

8:34 am

"TAKE A CHANCE ON Me" was on the stereo when Jo saw the reflection of the windshield dancing on the living room wall.

She's here. I wonder what this is going to be like. It's been so long. I wonder if she still talks as much as she used to? Will we still have anything in common?

Funny how time has managed to separate us, the once inseparable.

She hadn't seen her since her father's funeral, and it had only been a brief "I'm so sorry" with a quick hug. She thought of their last real parting, the day she caught the plane in Little Rock. Once choices had been made, and life was underway, the contact and friendship fizzled.

Time, and two completely different life choices.

She clearly remembered the impish grin Gina wore so often during those last years of high school.

Will she still be the same old Gina I remember?

There was only one way to know… Jo opened the door.

AUTHOR AND WRITER, NATALIE R VICE has spent a lifetime preparing for the stories created in *The Scrapbook Series*. A collection of stories focused on the lives of Jo and Gina, two women raised in the Ozark Mountains of northern Arkansas. She draws upon her life experiences as a young woman raised in small town America for the funny and sometimes dysfunctional adventures of the characters as they come together for the pursuit of lost friendship and new adventures.

Born in 1965, on an Air Force Base, her parents returned to the small town way of life to live and raise their 3 children. Natalie has spent most of her life within a 50 mile radius of that same small town, observing and finding humor in the everyday "mishaps" that occur when life is lived in a small town.

She has been an author, blogger and freelance writer for well over a decade and holds a Bachelor of Science in Accounting. In addition to creating *The Scrapbook Series*, she also offers services for the business, finance and education industries.

In 1977, at the TG&Y in Fayette, Al, I bought a plaque of an old Irish proverb/prayer. One of those lines reads:

Take time to dream, it is hitching your wagon to a star.

I still have the plaque; it hangs on my office wall and I still take time to dream. In following the dream of writing, I created the characters of Jorja Felsenthal and Regina Ingram and began their story.

THE SCRAPBOOK SERIES IS an opportunity to look at life through the eyes of the most unsung hero in American life: the everyday, average woman. We take life as it comes and find a way to deal with unbelievable situations: we laugh, we cry, we struggle. We get angry and frustrated. We are overjoyed and in tears simultaneously. We love in ways that are sometimes completely insane, and we reach for each other…. we reach for our girl friends. In doing so, we reach for a better tomorrow, while we learn to make the most of today.

To steal a phrase from Jackson Browne's *Everyman,* I wanted to create the "everywoman" in Jo and Gina. I wanted my readers to be able to identify with their life experiences. To read about one of their predicaments and say "Ah, yes. Been there done that."

I needed to be able to write about things, events and people that I was comfortable with. In my writings, although none of these characters are real, they were created from many of my own life experiences, interactions, thoughts, and beliefs. I needed to write in ways that provided a connection between myself, my work, and my readers.

I am a woman, so I wrote about women.

I have lived life and made mistakes, made the best of it and moved on. So have Jo and Gina.

As I wrote about their low moments, I cried. As I wrote about their funny escapades, I laughed. I want my readers to feel those same emotions. I want them to walk away from the story of Jo and Gina empowered as a woman, with hope in their heart and joy for tomorrow!

Below, I've included the Old Irish Proverb in its entirety. I hope it brings all of you as much inspiration as it always has to me.

Take time to work, it is the price of success.

Take time to think, it is the source of power.

Take time to play, it is the secret to perpetual youth.

Take time to read, it is the foundation of wisdom.

Take time to be friendly, it is the road to happiness.

Take time to dream, it is hitching your wagon to a star.

Take time to love and to be loved, it is the privilege of the gods.

Take time to look around, the day is too short to be selfish.

Take time to laugh, it is the music of the soul.

Women of the Ozarks,
Scrapbook Series…

Book X, A Prequel

NATALIE R. VICE

Can friendship last a lifetime?

Everyone says that hindsight is 20/20. If that's true, how much of that image in the rear view affects who we are today, or who we will become tomorrow?

Jo Felsenthal and Gina Ingram were the closest of childhood friends back in Polk Ridge, Arkansas. Growing up in this beautiful, close-knit Ozark community, they were surrounded by love and laughter.

But as these girls grew into women, choices were made, and life took them in very different directions.

Now, they're just hours away from a reunion several decades in the making. A out-of-the-blue Facebook "friend" request has snowballed into a face-to-face meeting. Both women are dealing with mixed emotions—excitement, nostalgia, and more than a little apprehension.

In *Memories of Tomorrow*, Jo and Gina weave their way through childhood memories and difficult life choices. They ponder how to cross over all their yesterdays to the girls they once were. Can they find anything in common after so many years spent living such different lives?

If you like The Sometimes Sister and Hurricane Season, you'll love the *Women of the Ozarks Scrapbook Series*.

Book One

Two separate paths. One enduring friendship.

Jo Felsenthal and Gina Ingram were girls of the '60s and '70s and grew into young women during one of the most turbulent social times in American history. The cultural forces of those tumultuous times had a tremendous impact on the choices they made and the women they became. As these two women, now in their fifth decade of life, look back to see just how far they've come, they long for the friendship they once shared.

Having traveled the world for nearly forty years as a military officer and NSA liaison, Jo Felsenthal is now forced to take a step backward and return to her childhood home of Polk Ridge, Arkansas. Stepping back into this old (and mostly forgotten) territory comes with its challenges. Her mom's health is failing, her career and personal life are in freefall, and she hasn't connected with anyone in Polk Ridge in a lifetime.

Gina Phillips has spent a lifetime facing more adversity than she cares to recall. From teenage mom, to widow, to social worker, she has made her way and her life in Polk Ridge, one of the poorest towns in one of the poorest counties in Arkansas. So when Gina decides unwind on her back porch after work, she's more than surprised when a familiar, yet long neglected friend pops up in her Facebook feed. Yet there she is: Jo! Gina's dearest childhood friend—now a complete stranger—is back in town. Her quick click on "friend request" is about to have lasting consequences….

Can these women find a way to bridge a lifetime of separation and recapture the friendship of their youth? They'll soon find out if a bucket full of childhood memories is enough to reignite a once-treasured friendship long abandoned. Set in a beautiful, close-knit Ozark community, *Tomorrow's Promise* is a story of family and friendship. Through joy and despair, Jo and Gina will walk you down a nostalgic road and perhaps into a promising future. If you like The Book Club and The Summer Girls, you'll love the *Women of the Ozarks Scrapbook Series.*

Book Two

NATALIE R. VICE

How Much of Your Future Depends on Your Past?

After decades apart, childhood friends Jo Felsenthal and Gina Ingram spend their first summer together after more than forty years. A few weeks spent revisiting life as the girls they used to be and getting to know each other as the women they've become has shown them that time and circumstances have changed them both.

They're different women with different ideals and different convictions. Gina has spent her life in their hometown of Polk Ridge, Arkansas, nestled in the Ozark mountains as a counselor for the poor and drug addicted. She's sympathetic and open minded to others' hardships. Jo, by contrast, has lived her life in the military—an environment with a single-minded purpose and a demand for rigid discipline.

For Jo, blending back into a community that distrusts the very government she has spent her life defending, leaves her completely at odds with the people Gina seems to adore. When Jo meets Gina's friends Max and Maxine, she's thrown for a loop as these two conspiracy driven hippies challenge her beliefs about the government and law—all of which has shaped her into the woman she is today. Her instant dislike of Gina's friends suddenly threatens the newly reunited childhood friends.

In *Crossing Yesterday*, the second book in the *Women of the Ozarks Scrapbook Series*, Jo and Gina are forced to ask: Just how far apart can two people be and still find common ground?

If you like Beach House for Rent and The Book of Lost Friends, you'll love the *Women of the Ozarks Scrapbook Series*.

Book Three

NATALIE R. VICE

It's the stuff you *don't* see coming, that changes your life's path.

Throughout your life you learn to plan, prepare, and plan some more. You learn to cope with the expected. It's the stuff you don't see coming that can be your undoing. Jo Felsenthal and Gina Ingram's lives are no different.

When Gina's son has a child out of wedlock and she learns that her deceased husband also fathered an illegitimate child, her carefully constructed family life is turned inside out. Gina's longtime friend and sometime boyfriend Melvin, suddenly seems completely uninterested in her latest turn of events. If she has ever needed a friend, it's now.

Jo has her own set of issues. She's confronted with revisiting her feelings for Paul Collections, the high school sweetheart she couldn't make room for all those years ago. Jo also finds herself confronted with a sister that seems to be in the midst of a mid-life crisis and co-workers in the midst of a blossoming romance.

In the *Unraveling*, life's plans seem to be quickly dissolving. They had a path they wanted to follow. They were making careful preparations for that path. Now, it seems that everyone and everything is conspiring to turn the most carefully constructed plans upside down! How did it all get so complicated?

Suddenly, finding a lost friendship seems like the easiest part of their lives.

If you like Before We Were Yours and The Sisters Café, you'll love the *Women of the Ozarks Scrapbook Series*.

Book Four

NATALIE R. VICE

Recapturing love and a sense of adventure isn't as freeing as you would think…

Ready to take advantage of retirement, lifelong friends Jo Felsenthal and Gina Ingram plan a two-week trip to sunny California. In this new environment, far from home, the two women finally feel free to say and do what they want. Gina finds she's rather fond of pot and Jo re-discovers her love of wine. They finally understand the phrase, *California dreamin'*.

What was supposed to be a short trip, turns into months away from their home in the Ozarks. Gina begins to feel the increasing tug of her responsibilities at home in Polk Ridge, but is reluctant to leave her never-ending vacation in the Golden State.

Jo, on the other hand, has finally come to the staggering

revelation that she's once again fallen in love with teen sweetheart Paul Collections. This time, though, Paul isn't necessarily a free man.

As realities in their hometown of Polk Ridge, Arkansas keep calling, Jo and Gina find themselves trying to answer an age old question: Is the grass really any greener on the other side?

If you like The Sometimes Sister and Beach House for Rent, you'll love the *Women of the Ozarks Scrapbook Series.*

Book Five

The Fates giveth, and the Fates taketh away…

Almost a decade has passed since a fateful Facebook friend request brought childhood friends Jo Felsenthal and Gina Ingram back together after a life apart. The inseparable girls of '76 are now older, wiser, and best friends again. They've shared tears and laughter, anger and happiness, trials and triumphs. They have stopped searching for the girls they used to be and found lasting friendship in the women they have become.

Jo has rekindled a once-lost love and Gina has reconciled herself with life in the Ozarks. The girl who once had no idea which path to choose, has found that the path has chosen her. The mountains, the people, and the family Gina has fought so hard to hold together have given her the sweetest gift of all: enduring love.

Jo and Gina's friendship has been tried and tested for almost half a century. Together, they have experienced girlish dreams and desires, love and loss, happiness and regrets. But most importantly they've grown into women who cherish a lasting friendship.

Then fate deals their enduring friendship one final blow...

Wait For Me, is the fifth and final book in the Women Of The Ozarks Scrapbook Series, and will share the poignant final stories of two women who have seen so much and found friendship through it all.